The Barnyard Bake Off

by **Katie Dale**

illustrated by
Chiara Fiorentino

One baking hot morning, Henrietta was
pulling up carrots when Lulu walked by.

"Hi Henrietta!" called Lulu.

"Do you want to play?"

"Not now, I'm gathering carrots," said Henrietta. "It's hard work – would you like to help?"

6

At lunchtime, Sally slithered by.

"Hi Henrietta! Do you want to play?"

she hissed.

"Not now, I'm mixing batter,"

said Henrietta. "It's hard work –

would you like to help?"

That afternoon, Billy buzzed by.

"Hi Henrietta, do you want to play?"

he called.

"Not now, I'm rolling icing,"

said Henrietta. "It's hard work –

would you like to help?"

All day Henrietta dug and baked
and decorated.

Finally, her cake was ready.

The delicious smell spread far and wide.

"Sorry," replied Henrietta. "I'm entering it in the Great Barnyard Bake Off contest tonight!"

The Great Barnyard Bake Off?

THE GREAT BARNYARD BAKE OFF!
Judged by Chef Ram-See!
Tonight at 6:00pm

But then, Henrietta slippped!

OH NO!

It's RUINED!

"There isn't time!" Henrietta wailed.

"The contest starts in an hour!"

17

An hour later, Henrietta looked at the other cakes sadly.

"Welcome to the Great Barnyard Bake Off contest!" said Chef Ram-See.

Sniff!

Chef Ram-See tasted and judged cakes

of all different shapes and sizes.

But the last cake of all looked very odd indeed.
Henrietta gasped. For beside the cake stood
Lulu, Billy and Sally! Had they entered the
contest too?

We call it
Eat 'n' Mess!

Everyone held their breath as Chef Ram-See took a big bite...

"Absolutely delicious!"

Chef Ram-See cried.

"This is the best cake I have ever tasted! Congratulations! You three are our best bakers! You win the prize!"

Everyone cheered.

"Oh no, we didn't make the cake," said Henrietta's friends. "We just decorated it."

I made the cream!

I picked the flowersss.

I drizzled the honey!

But Henrietta baked the wonderful cake!

"Congratulations, Henrietta!" Chef Ram-See cried. Everyone cheered as he gave Henrietta the prize.

Henrietta beamed. It was the happiest day

of her life. Not just because Chef Ram-See

thought she was the best baker...

...but because she had the best friends.

Thank you, Lulu, Sally and Billy!

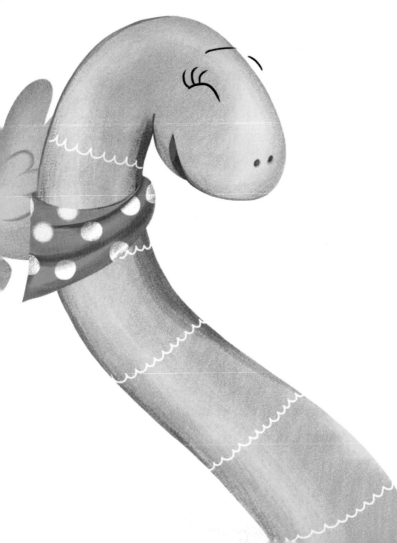

Quiz

1. At first, why didn't Lulu, Sally or Billy help Henrietta make the cake?
a) They don't like cake
b) It was hard work
c) They were making their own cakes

2. How did Henrietta ruin her cake?
a) She sat on it
b) She ate it
c) She slipped

3. Who judged the Great Barnyard Bake Off?
a) Chef Sheep-See
b) Chef Ram-See
c) Chef Goat-See

4. How did Henrietta's friends help?

a) They baked a new cake

b) They decorated her cake

c) They gave her a surprise party

5. Why did Henrietta's cake win?

a) It tasted the best

b) It looked the best

c) It smelt the best

Turn over for answers

Book Bands for Guided Reading

The Institute of Education book banding system is a scale of colours that reflects the various levels of reading difficulty. The bands are assigned by taking into account the content, the language style, the layout and phonics. Word, phrase and sentence level work is also taken into consideration.

Maverick Early Readers are a bright, attractive range of books covering the pink to white bands. All of these books have been book banded for guided reading to the industry standard and edited by a leading educational consultant.

To view the whole Maverick Readers scheme, visit our website at
www.maverickearlyreaders.com

Or scan the QR code above to view our scheme instantly!

Quiz Answers: 1b, 2c, 3b, 4b, 5a